Pink X-Ray

Poems and Stories

by
Brad Rose

ISBN: 978-0-9908413-5-7

Printed in the United States of America

This book is a work of fiction. The characters, names and plot are entirely a product of the author's imagination. Any resemblance of the characters or incidents in the book to real life persons or events is unintentional and purely coincidental.

Grateful acknowledgment is made to the editors of the journals and anthologies who first published some of the poems contained in this book, earlier versions of which appeared in: *The Baltimore Review, Boston Literary Magazine, Camroc Press Review, Cease Cows, The Common Line Journal, Centrifugal Eye, Heavy Feather Review, Future Cycle Poetry, The Los Angeles Times, MadHat Lit, The Molotov Cocktail, Off the Coast, Posit, The Potomac, Right Hand Pointing, riverbabble, San Pedro River Review, Six Sentences, Sleetmagazine, Tattoo Highway, Third Wednesday,* and *Uut Poetry,*

Front Cover Image: Aspireimages
Cover Design: Hannah Rose
Back Cover Photo: Hannah Rose
Interior Photo: *Deliverance* used with permission from the artist

Big Table Publishing Company
Boston, MA
www.bigtablepublishing.com

"The function of the imagination is not to make strange things settled; so much as it is to make settled things strange."

~ GK Chesterton

TABLE OF CONTENTS

I.

II.

III.

I.

Veterans' Benefits

Sky full of ghosts,
a war in mind,
I hear tactical voices.
Been discharged three years,
feel empty as a vacant apartment.
Still got fumes in my blood.
Sometimes, I hear fizzing, too,
like positive and negative leads, touching,
feel like I'm breathing nails.

Before she left,
my wife said she started to dream
my nightmares,
said she's seen brighter eyes
in the faces of the dead.

Now, my car is my living room.
Got Rhode Island plates,
smallest state in the union.
Can barely see it on aerial recon.

I pull into the parking lot of this Cineplex,
put on my night-vision goggles.
Even if my blood's been hypnotized,
no one can find me. Not here.
I wait for a while,
tune the car radio to the designated station,
decipher the grey, static hum.

A good Marine, I await further orders.

Note to Self

I am my own equivalent.
I'm named after myself.
I'm someone who's memorized a secret vocabulary
to describe the future.
I believe the world is alphabetical,
that it's moving unstoppably from A to Z.
Of course, I have to remind myself
that we see only the hands of the clock,
not time, itself,
and that no matter how far we go,
it's just the distance traveled,
but there are so many directions
it's difficult to know which way to proceed.
You can stand perfectly still,
but the commotion is your head
is a red radio
playing all the blue songs, at once,
a box of nails nailed to a wall of boxes.

Once, I got mad at my friend.
It happened in a car.
It was an accident.
I didn't mean for it to happen,
but it did.
Most things happen that way.
Even music, even death.

Did you know that hummingbirds sing?
They sing to themselves.
You can't hear them,
I can't hear them,
but they sing, anyway.

It's like attending the funeral of someone
you don't know.
You're sorry they're dead,
but you can't cry,
you can't shed a tear,
unless they're someone
who reminds you of someone.
Then you cry.
You cry your eyes out
because you can't help it.
You cry because they remind you
of someone who reminds you
of you.

Tehachapi Seven Eleven

Wedged between the customers and the Marlboros,
I'm stationed at the register,
cans of Red Man, Copenhagen, Durango, and Rooster, a scrim behind me.
Salt-sweet jerky sticks stuffed in a cookie jar,
cash in the drawer,
lottery tickets draped like flags of fictitious countries.
Scratch and win.
Outside, in the heat, the pumps line-up, white and blue,
black hoses, akimbo.
A gallon of gas costs an hour's pay.
You can wash your car,
if you want, or drive off, dusty.

Thursday's my day-off.
I get up, get dressed,
the sun rises like a slow yawn,
There's a note still on the kitchen table.
It's in her handwriting:
Go fishing, it says.
Drain the lake to catch the fish.

The house is empty now.
She took both the kids. Neither of them was mine.
I wasn't the first one to notice her thirteen year-old,
sorry and pretty as a freshly painted bungalow,
little smudge of a smile.
The kind that runs toward trouble, not away.
I think about her.
It used to bother me, but not anymore.
You get used to it.

Force acting on an object,
speed of light, the same for everyone
gravity pulling everything down,

rod and reel, lure and bait.

Abandoned House

I want to get out of the car. And why shouldn't I? It's parked, isn't it? Outside a house. An abandoned house. I like abandoned houses. I like to look at them. This one sends me a silent message. It's tired. Tired of being in this world. Fixed to the earth, it's tired of this house-world. This one wants to get plastic surgery, become a theme park, move to Florida. Hey, that reminds me. Maybe I'll look you up. Yeah, I'm going to look you up. Are you still in the world? Do you have a house? I saw King Tut's sarcophagus, once. In a museum. Gold, calm, still. Face of a girl. Nothing inside. Like a dream of deep space. Did you know that sleep is the third leading cause of death? Even if you don't like to think about it–even when you're driving through a tunnel– sleep is death. King Tut looked quiet as a river. Asleep, calm, dreaming, with his eyes wide open. Something seemed to float there, just above his quiet stare. I'll bet if he uncrossed his arms, he could have reached out, touched it. But the weight of that gold weighed heavy on Tut. He lay there, steady, motionless. He wasn't going anywhere. I wonder if he was tired? Tired of staring. Tired of dreaming. When I get out of this car, I'm going to go inside that house. I'm going to look around. Maybe, see what emptiness looks like. From the inside. Maybe, look out the house's windows. Just look out the windows, think about all those rooms with no one in them. No one dreaming. I'll bet it's quiet in there. Quiet and empty. Like a dream. Like a god.

Honey Gets Her Wish

Like electrons darting stochastically about an atom's nucleus, the flies circle the victim's dead body–a noisy hum against the murder scene's otherwise grim silence. I hate this part of the job, but I steel myself, reach into the dead man's sharkskin suit-coat pocket, and remove his cell phone. Checking the phone's call history, I hit redial, and wait as the phone dials the last number the dead man called, only an hour earlier. A number accompanied solely by the name "Honey." Three rings, and a woman's furious voice commands, 'Don't you ever, ever, call me again." The phone goes dead.

March Snow at Arlington

The slow air, snow quiet,
salt-white flecks, descending
into this world's vacancy.
White silence seeping,
into the stilled mouths of the dead.

I wait here, for the lost,
the slumbering slain,
to storm their way home;
through the sand of their desert,
the snow of their death.

I see, beneath this earth,
in its obverse darkness,
a line of children, single-file,
each child smartly dressed,
shoes shined bright,
for the first day of school.

Quarry Lake

Cement-dry August. All day, I've studied my memories. The past will not apologize. It's a jeweler cutting stones, but not diamonds.

Underneath that misspelled tattoo, your smooth, bronze skin, a membrane of beauty.

On the phone, you declared, *This is not my life*, then hung up.

All those years I was afraid to swim in Quarry Lake, its anonymous bottom, like an unlit room, locked.

The police reported it as an accident. I know you were not afraid. Time running out, the underwater crew recovered you, just before their deadline.

Death Explained

it's music and it isn't
there's a small chance it's a circle
it can't be washed off
like sleeping underwater
the right and the wrong answer
easy to learn but difficult to master
black boomerang of cinematic technique
invisible ink
the same dark as in every tunnel
happens in no time
syllables of water
emptier than the moon's seas
night's black hunger for day, quenched
all its infinite hours contained in one sun
a knot loops through itself and tightens
climb back into your body
try again to explain it
try louder

An Apostate Visits the Temple of the Buddha

A murmur flowing out into the black bay of night,
where the stars bob, tiny, glittering boats,
adrift, anchorless.
When I peer up, through the perfumed smoke,
past the god's rolling belly, smooth as soap,
up into his oblivious face, with its once-painted eyes,
and his indifference to sin,
he seems to exhale, *good luck*,
not cynically, but as if he really means it.
When I look down at the temple floor,
its stone worn talc-smooth by supplication,
I can see that I've kneeled here
through one too many lives.

In Golden Gate Park

A cocoon of myself,
bundled in these minutes
that refuse to pass,
I have no idea what my address is.
Every day, in the same skin,
I come here to dream of something
that's more beautiful
for having once been broken.

The clinic says I think about things too much.
I ask how much is just enough?
Then I tell them I'm only thinking the thoughts I'm thinking,
not all the other ones.

Tuesday, I read in the newspaper
the Governor said the lethal injections aren't working,
that the prisoner's body shook like a marionette.
Wrapped in that story, I hardly slept Tuesday night.

Did you know people are less likely to flee
a hurricane with a woman's name, than a man's?
My ex-wife said I'm smart,
but I'm always solving the wrong problem.

Lightning is five times hotter than the sun.
It strikes the earth three million times a day.

I never sleep in the same place twice.

The Mug Shot Photographer

Full-face and profile, rumpled and blank,
they glare into the middle distance,
some with new mistakes' fresh pink scars,
others with the pimples of innocence.
Eyes, blue as a bruise or brown as dirt,
their faces, shallow, wild places,
like a bed where an animal might have slept
for one night.
Drunk hair spikes toward the florescent ceiling,
locker-room scent of fear and resignation,
they slouch against the yardstick's measure,
as I gauge their height, assay their stature.
Murderers, thieves,
spouse abusers, arsonists
each sinks like a tired fish
toward the murky bottom.
The taxidermist's docile prey.

I aim the zombie camera.
Art is of no use.
Not even a hand without fingerprints is guiltless.
At the end of each shift,
I take a selfie.

Burnt Ghosts

Carbon dark, invisible as fish in the rain,
what good are our tattoos?
No one can see them.
Disconnected phone numbers,
who would ever call us?

Frictionless, flame-smooth,
one degree above freezing,
we weigh less than ourselves.
It can't be explained.
Dark matter, unseen as salt on snow.

At the door, you can't quite tell if we are coming or going.
We pause for a posthumous cigarette
and watch the smoke rise in reverse,
our brilliant enthusiasms, difficult to discern,
our dark designs, undetectable.

Tonight, we drive out to Queens.
The houses, deserts
folded in on themselves,
waiting for something colorful to happen.
This is where the world is.

Every 45 seconds in America,
a house catches fire.

Weather permitting.

Safety Dancing for the Recovering Arsonist

I've learned to dance, legally, although sometimes fun can really throw you off track. I've sorted through gravity, that selfish force that clutches everything closer, as it tears it apart. Now, I dance only the officially approved, non-gyrational dances: the Pressed Soup, the Unclear Disorder, and the Loyal Remedy. Practicing in front of the mirror, while I'm alone, at home, I swoop and swoon in a low, thin zoom. My legs, provocative chopsticks, my arms, a theater of centrifugal force. There's something friendly about my convulsive movements, a happy blur of brightness in a stone gray fog. Of course, no matter how careful you are, there's no avoiding the second law of human combustion: whenever you dance, strike a match, set the house ablaze. I love the music of approaching sirens. Some people say dance is a language. My dancing speaks for itself.

Everything Happens for a Reason

I'm studying for my polygraph test. It's not one of those easy, multiple-choice tests. You have to be smarter than the internet; you have to know bee logic, know exactly where to land. I don't think they're going to grade my exam on a curve. But, I'm not worried. I'm a great test-taker. I got an A+ on my marksman's exam. The day I took that test, I wore a t-shirt that said "Gun Control" on the front. On the back, it said, "SQUEEZE, Don't Pull." The boys at the shooting range thought that was hoot. Fortunately, I look good when I'm dressed in camouflage. When I get down on the ground, you can't really tell it's me. I look like a desert with leaves blowing over it. Vicki used to say I looked like the wind, with its boots on. She was a million laughs. I told her it's all about rightsizing. You've got to get it just right; not too much, not too little. That's why I used to carry one of those yellow tape measures with me wherever I went. But I don't need them anymore. I've gotten pretty good at guessing how big or small things are. It's all about perspective. Vicki used to say it's a God-given talent. I can guess the carats of diamonds and the caliber of bullets. I could guess your collar size, right now. No sweat. My lawyer says there's a lot riding on this trial. He said my neck is on the line. I told him that when I'm on the stand, I'll sit quiet as a pearl, my face, hard as an oyster shell. When they ask me those questions, I'm going to be ready. Like an ambush. Like I'm firing into the kill zone. Cool and controlled. Squeeze, don't pull. Hug, don't strangle. Even if Vicki's mom and dad are in the courtroom, even if I'm convicted, I'm cool, I'm ready. Like they say, everything happens for a reason. Well, almost everything.

A Passenger

Urges prowl and posture
digging a deeper ditch
through your delicate frame.
You are seven miles of oblivion,
secrets too large to detect,
darker than swallowed mountains.

Nerves, a cul de sac,
stitches jittering in a pale paradise,
something is almost left of your heart.
Without an enemy, you'd disappear.
Like a list, you write yourself down,
so you won't forget.
Dire candy, too many dead to remember,
accidents don't just happen,
they require practice.

I could be a cure.
You take me only
in controlled doses.
You love the way I love you,
always, not forever.

Heavy weather now,
sky squeezing down,
as the taxi, a supplicant,
crawls toward you.

Get in, you bark,
Give the driver the address.

Rouge Canoe

Just the two of us, boy and girl,
out in the rouge canoe,
mid-bay smooth as a pressed shirt,
yet current insistent at our hull,
when you toss our paddles overboard
and grin as they drift away,
Now, how will we ever get back?

The shore a mile off
I recall, as I always do in open water
Breughel's Icarus
and Auden's later limning
of our obliviousness to all fates
except our own,

but it's not that serious, I know.
I'll dive in to retrieve the paddles
or we'll hail a boater to tow us in,
and once ashore, you'll say,
I'm sure glad we had lifejackets,
but I know you'll later paint a picture for your friends
of something that happened out there,
not quite a drowning,
an incident, nonetheless,
requiring a boy's fall,
witnesses or not.

A Prisoner of Love

It was an understandable mistake. A small figurine of a girl, you were available only in stores that sold bullets. It was like a silent movie. Thank goodness, it was a lot better than it sounded. Of course, love can't be attributed entirely to crop failure. Your kiss was far less frigid than lipstick on a snow cone. Your mother said ours was a love inspired by an actual event based on a real Hollywood movie. When you introduced me to her, she turned to your Dad and yelled, *Morey, I'm warning you, don't put those two electric eels in the same tank.* I kept thinking, is this going to be on the final exam? But you were so reassuring. You seemed happy as an emoticon. And you looked so Parisian, too. I couldn't stop myself from blurting out, *I lake you a leetle beet.* (Isn't that amazing? I don't even speak French.) When I whispered to you, *Today is the first day of the rest of our week*, you replied, *Thank God, I know shorthand.* Sadly, I soon learned that fog is much harder to plow than snow. Evidently, sometimes Cupid stumbles while on his fool's errand. Like a waxed toboggan, things went downhill, lickity split. You ran off with another parolee. But I soon caught up with you. You said it was the way I looked at other women, especially my three polygamous wives. How many times did I have to tell you, it's not true if you don't say it out loud?

The Distant Shooting I Hear Reminds Me of the Boys in Marketing

It's the regional marketing managers' meeting, again. Same as last year, visual Muzak scratching itself against the hum and hiss of the crowd's cosmic background microwave radiation. The room is big, like a cat eating a mouse. An indecisive tide, I drift in and out. I'm groomed like a two-way mirror viewed in black light: sometimes you see me, sometimes you don't. When the production figures are unveiled, they beam bright as a Broadway marquee (thank you China, thank you Bangladesh.) A small crowd gathers up front to reload the PowerPoint bullets, to cheer-on the killing we'll make. A war cry rises from the cauldron of corporate happy talk. It builds to a catchy, brutish crescendo. Sally whoops, *I'd forgive a helluvalota ugly, for some really good country music, right now.* The mounting rhythm of the crowd makes me want to recite from the *People's Hymnbook of Automaton Shouts.* I feel tiny as an insect's sleep. The Sales department fires Bible verses back and forth, while Marketing pummels Sales. Bill leans over to me and hisses *There's no turning back now, Carl.* I smile my glibbest sales force simper, and meander vaguely to the back of the pulsing bildungsroman. I light a blue electronic cigarette, bat away the legerdemain smoke. If only I could launch a reverse jihad, an uphill avalanche, but it's hopeless. All I can see approaching is a lurking incident betting on an ingenious accident. What are the chances? The prospects look darker than tunnel work. Maybe I'm blindfolded? Maybe I tripped a silent alarm? Maybe I'm a miraculous clone captive to a wicked consensus? All I want to do is shout mysterious farewells, to growl unspeakable verbs. (Man, I could really go for some good Canadian food, right now.) I have no idea what we're selling. Maybe I've glimpsed the future's shining hereafter, the extinction of its anticipated past. It's a colossal machine raving its death-slackened grin in my direction. I see it lumbering toward me, sleek as a diamond—polished, glittering, taut. On its implacable frame, clean as red nipple,

I see a trigger—a single trigger. It beckons. It teases. It whispers. It lures. *For heaven's sake, Cleveland, whatever you do, don't pull it.*

.

Two Buds at Cotillion

She was as out of place at the Dallas Cotillion as Christmas lights shining brightly in a mid-July day. She couldn't dance. She couldn't mingle. She didn't have a proper date. In fact, she'd snuck in, alone, through the catering entrance, after having read an article the week before, about this posh soiree in one of those swank, metropolitan magazines that are read almost exclusively by lawyers, high society Texas matrons, and sparkling blonde debutants (named either Ashley, Haley or Heather.) Now, standing at the bar, alone as a prickly saguaro, she's surrounded by elegant couples sipping green-apple martinis and cooing to one another about their planned Paris excursions. She soothes herself with two cans of Budweiser: one crumpled in each clenched fist.

Perfect Background Music

How does one build a robot snake, like the Little Mermaid, but with different kinds of scales, and a tail with a rattle? I've studied elastic statues, and I can assure you, skin is of no use. I want to lie down, like a prairie, in low, flat, sleep, my eyes relics of rain. I can't be certain if these words are eroticized upholstery or upholstered eroticism? Despite all this anti-gravity, it occurs to me that I'll probably never record a dance album. Like a bug on its back, I just can't seem to get any traction. Guess what. The sky learns to be blue. Like skywriting, it takes a lot practice, and no clouds. You may ask, "What readies us for living?" One-third of suicides don't leave a note. Illiteracy remains a huge problem in the world today. The anger of misunderstood alphabets, like raging houses, their roofs fuming in the blue air, lawns crackling like a fireplace. They say a certain party has flammable parents. But then, they say a lot of things. Don't you think noisy weather makes perfect background music. Especially lightning. As you leave, please, don't forget to turn off the stove, lock the front door, bring the matches.

Not Enough Bullets

Knife-cold bones, refrigerator white
skeleton gets out of the car
saunters toward me
the fog of tar black thoughts
spilling from his skull
like moonlight through a broken window
squeezes narrow his little stray-dog eyes
and says to me
Nothingness is symmetrical, man
but I'm not convinced
so he jitters a jagged-bone jig
to prove he's dead
and seen the other side
wherein he knows of what he speaks
and through a bolt of black bone holes
indented in a saw toothed smile
adds, *Know what I mean?*
But I don't
so he says
One part's exactly the same as any other
and I wonder why he's telling me this
because the dead don't often speak to me
except once before
when from our fever-twisted sheets
you looked up
and said, *I know you wish I were dead you bastard*
but even if you wanted to
you couldn't kill me because I'm dead already

thanks to you
and no matter how much you want to
you can't kill me twice you bastard.

Not enough bullets.

Ken Plans a Trip to Toys "R" Us

Your long, beautiful legs, candy kiss smile—almost too perfect. My million dollar valentine, your ideas of perfection were far from flawless. Voicemails unanswered, I stopped by Wednesday, after work, to find your lifeless body buried up to your blonde shoulders in the Easy-Bake oven. Oh, my sweet, sweet Barbie, whose life were you really living, anyway? Your sherbet-pink jeep, parked in your dream house garage, forever and ever. How will I ever replace you?

Visiting Los Angeles' National Veterans' Cemetery, Westwood California

I jump the fence,
walk on graves.
I'm infantry.
Listening for angry helicopters,
I expect something to arrive,
maybe by satellite.
My hair is laughing.
For a long time now, the nightmares.
Like the dead, they don't behave like they should,
but you never know.
It takes time.
I'm learning to work with gravity
not against it.
My name is written in ball point pen
on the bottom of both my shoes.
I've learned to dodge lightning strikes.
My stunt double says I'm lucky
psychiatry is just drugs.
Says I have a custodial smile.
Today, I took the blue pill.
I must be swimming with my clothes on.
My arms are heavy as railway tracks.
I hear red sirens approaching,
fire three warning shots into the air.

Yes sir, I promise,
that's as close as I'll ever get
to the sky.

II.

Rattlers

Outside Mojave, the sky suddenly clouded, as if someone had shut off an immense blue valve, and ferocious clouds scraped in, low and gray, toward us. The scent of creosote and mesquite syruped the air, but the rain refused to find a place to fall.

The two of us, tighter than a tourniquet, sat in the car and traded serried accusations, like switchbacks plummeting into a deep ravine.

Who had cheated on whom, first?

Then, as we got out of the car and made our way toward the trailhead, you barked, "Watch your step, there might be rattlers," but you caught yourself and began to sing, "California, Here I Come," in a kind of snide shivaree, embarrassed that you had let your guard down, if only for a moment, and shown any care for me at all.

Peering down at the seemingly vacant sand, I began to quietly count my footsteps, in a self-soothing mantra—just in case it turned out you were right.

I Drive to North Carolina the Day After the Execution of My Wife's Murderer

Red, wet, drops smear the arc
of the windshield's murmuring blades.

It's raining ants.

Otherwise, the glass is clear
as drinking water,

except for a thousand tiny legs,
flinching phantom limbs,
waving at me.

You know how it is.

Well, it isn't like that.

It's different.

Oh, How I Almost Loved You

Most of the time, we couldn't tell that we were moving,
bodies, fog-slow, quiet as stone,
bed, still as a lawn.
Like Swiss neutrality, nothing happened.

There are 7 billion people in the world.
I am either one of them, or a mime.
To mow the yard, I yearn to set the grass ablaze.
Instead, I run out of gasoline.

In all the old movies about the Arctic
someone always warns,
Don't go to sleep,
you'll freeze to death.

In my head, I do the numbers:
thermometer jibs at absolute zero.
Is it any wonder I didn't have a career in magic?
Thank you for your patience.

Horse Fly

Black, gasoline-in-water iridescence,
five thousand emerald eyes,

when I try to swat him,
he bolts and parries,

avoids my slo-mo ambition,
my pathetic, molasses motion.

Nimbly dodging my feeble newspaper smack,
he eyes me from across the room,

whinnies.

The Last to Know

I love you.
But I don't know it.

The frenzied bees sting themselves,
their yellow screams, so piercing,
they don't notice.

Hatchet Job

Her departure was as final as a stone placed over a newly closed grave. I should have seen it coming. A week before she left to return to her husband, she cut her own hair, using only a butcher's knife and no mirror.

Six months passed and I got up enough nerve to phone her--not from our old apartment, of course, but from a pay phone outside a Bar we used to drink in, together on the East Side, called Capone's. She answered the phone, but hung up the second I said her name... didn't even give me a chance to say hello.

That's what really killed me.

Snowman

Black button eyes
blind as a stump,
two rolled bellies
crammed tight with ice,
your chalk white skin
fell out of the sky
into a world of another's making.
A single element is the God you know.
Now that you're here,
what pleasure is yours?

Tonight is darker than the rest,
its chill soothes your bitter, blue ache.
Hold me tenderly in your arms
until the wind tears down your knife-drawn smile,
until you've seen through this white-dark world.

Last Night at the Holiday Inn

The rain patters on the roof, like soft applause. I'm listening, closely. Very closely. Constant acceleration. You can hear the sky, swarming, shivering. Listen. Low altitude velocity. Before I know it, it's just like fun. But harder to enjoy. In the next room, I hear laughter, like a little boat, bobbing. Just laughter. And at the end of my bed, my suitcase, small as a monosyllable. I'm visiting. Only visiting. I can't stay. Really, I can't. Goedel's incompleteness theorem. Always something missing. The letter *J* is not in the periodic table. What am I waiting for? Something tells me, it could get ugly. Something tells me shut up and concentrate. Something keeps telling me. Everything is ticking, the wallpaper, the air conditioner, the rain. Sharp, bright, ticking. I'm listening. It ticks faster. Nine bullets. By the time you read this, everything will be different. Nine Bullets. What am I waiting for? Faster. No, faster. Everything will be different.

The Next Thing You Know

Everything, its own invention, happens eventually, although sometimes not at all: the music of fog, cannibal piñata, razor blade hula hoops. Have you noticed that if you talk about time, it slows? If you talk about love, it stops? Today, in Mecca, it's 109 and raining arithmetic bees. The sky has gone too far. Clocks are machines for the manufacture of moments. Time is its own décor. I wonder what color I should paint the red ant farm? As the smoke clears, my body is riddled with PowerPoint bullets. Fortunately, I'm never hungry, because I'm food. Loving you is like chewing bees to get honey. The newspaper reads itself and sobs uncontrollably. I'm happy that I'm a room all to myself. I leave things to chance; nothing is ever my fault. Beneath the striped fur of the tiger, the skin, too, is striped.

Naked to the Waist

It wasn't summer, it was heaven. I'd always wondered if death and life were the same, did angels get exhausted from flapping their wings? Sis said it wasn't true that Eve was made from earth and bone and salty Mississippi backwater. I told her Adam loved Eve, the way Pa loved Ma. She asked me if that was before or after they were cast out of the garden? I said *both*.

The smooth warm ooze of the Mississippi, God in that sunlight. Pa, lost in last spring's flood.

Deliverance, oil on canvas, Theresa Elliot

Las Vegas Jackpot

Outside *Caesar's*, sudden, pummeling, hail
falls like stolen coins
clattering on the roof of a cathedral.
We look up at the thunderhead,
hear only the lucky music of our laughter.

The Snow Leopard

Every thing is two things, simultaneously. This is due to the multiplier effect: firefly, lovehate, stopwatch, cowboy, Iceland. Of course, there are a number of ways to think "snow." Don't think Dalmatian, Holstein, Rorschach, ladybug; nor zebra stripe, bumble bee, tiger shark, barber pole. Think Admiral Bird. Bird claimed he reached both the North and South Poles, where he discovered the Holy Ghost, the vacant page, the lost horizon, the avant-garde. Although these claims have been disputed–most convincingly by indigenous peoples who insist they discovered Admiral Bird–there is no doubt that these milestones were both particles and waves. That said, some things are never quite themselves, no matter how unified they appear. For example, we must never ask, "Is Schrodinger's cat dead or alive?" Rather, "What is the greatest probability that Kitty merely naps?" Can diamonds really be a girl's best friend? Is it illegal in Oklahoma to hunt whales? There is no such thing as time, yet the moment perpetually approaches. In this soulless night, a black jaguar stalks us, its methodical breathing an omen of its immaculate intention. When it draws close enough for us to hear its low growl, to smell its feral scent, you'll see its black coat is composed of smoky rosettes. Think nothing of it. With a 910 kilogram-force, the jaguar's jaws clench twice as tightly as those of the snow leopard. God sings a song so beautiful, even He can't hear it.
Listen.

Second Cousins

The night, a dark manifesto, stars in riot,
heading toward themselves and back.
Coffin-black beach, where our shadows would lie down,
if they could.
You and I, blessed only by what we want,
hunting it down, hoping it will pass,
knowing it won't.
We've lived these lives, beautiful with mistakes,
certain only of that which is broken.
Tonight we know precisely
what brings us to this late shore.

Prime numbers, divisible
only by one, and ourselves,
we listen to the breakers,
their tongues shivering toward us,
and imagine the mute fish,
their silver blades darting invisibly
beneath unsummoned waves.
The sky, an enormous room,
sea breathing beneath its bent ceiling,
hem of the horizon too sunken to see.
Ours is the lowest passageway.

Bend and buckle, warp and twist,
until we are swept still as these dunes.

The tide flows.

It returns.

It never stops.

The Scream

Next to the Oslofjord, at sunset,
Munch went for a walk and was moved
to create The Scream.
Word of mouth?
Indeed it is, but you'd never know it.
We are more than ready to receive the sea,
a guest, not a passenger.
The rose-red city, half as old as time,
worthy of the most spoiled sultan.
The word, hanging in the air,
mixed with the scent of burning ashes.
Could today be the day?
After a day of sightseeing,
some people create poetry
without ever picking up a pen.
What is bare life?
Think, for a moment, of the kind of crowd
you see swarming around an all-you-can-eat buffet,
in Las Vegas.
Make it yours.

Make it yours.
In Las Vegas,
you see, swarming around, an all-you-can-eat buffet.
Think, for a moment, of the kind of crowd.
What is bare life?
Without ever picking up a pen,
some people create poetry,
after a day of sightseeing.
Could today be the day?

Mixed with the scent of burning ashes,
the word, hanging in the air,
worthy of the most spoiled sultan.

The rose-red city, half as old as time,
a guest, not a passenger.
We are more than ready to receive the sea.
Indeed, it is, but you'd never know it,
word of mouth.
To create The Scream and be moved,
Munch went for a walk,
next to the Oslofjord, at sunset.

A Stabbing

Changed my prints, moved eleven times, learned to blend in with the crowd. But there's always something coming, no matter how good you get at looking over your shoulder.

In my front pocket, I worry the rosary of two copper-tipped bullets. At 42ND St., a man with a scar scrawled across his forehead approaches. As he nears, his fog-gray eyes meet mine. I'm dead certain I can hear him ticking.

"Don't be ridiculous," I reassure myself, *"bombs don't tick."*

What I Heard from the Girl Who Tends Bar at "The Blackboard"

Like an asylum orderly,
I've heard a lot of things.
Tonight, the girl behind the bar
is the girl in the music.
Blue Novocain, her eyes could numb the sun.
Between riots of roistering rockabilly,
she bends across the bar, whispers something to me
that sounds like rain falling on a cinerarium.
She can't wait to get off work.
At 2:00, we drive to her house.
She's silent as a stone.
I have the best taste in the worst music.
Behind the wheel, I emulate the perfect me.
We stop by her ex's place,
children's toys asleep on the dark lawn.
I feel light as confetti,
lower than a hanged man's shoes.
She opens the car door, slips out.
The night's green scent squeezes in.
What could go wrong? she laughs back at me,
Keep the car running.
As she disappears into the dim mouth of the house,
the sky kneels closer to the street's stooped roofs.
Then, like a child's fist pummeling a pillow,
muted shots describe the unthinkable.
I'll never un-hear those bullets' blunt report.

Shaving Mirror

The end was always at hand, only today, more so. When she walked out, he discovered that everything remained the same, nothing changed. Confounded, he waited for a breakthrough, or a breakdown. Neither came. Just the bills piling up, week after week, like layers of earth shoveled into the open grave of someone he almost recognized. That morning, when he cut himself while shaving, only the mirror bled.

I am a Telephone

The dog barked all morning.
The green trees breathed blue air.

I'm resting now, on the motel bed,
the TV watching me.

I am a telephone.
Why don't you call?

Blood-black night in my veins,
I want one good noise,
so I turn on the radio's truth music.

When you wore your flammable party body
I wanted you, like charred bones want flesh.

I think I hear ringing, now,
I'm a phone call to myself.

Naked on this bed,
I have no address.

Wherever you've gone,
I will call you,
remind you
I'm not your fault.

They're Reading My Mind Again

I feel it when I'm asleep. Sometimes when I'm awake, too. Those damn magnetic fields. My girlfriend, Raylene, says I should relax. I tell her it's hard to relax when you're in Demolition. It makes you jumpy. Especially when you're on the thirteenth floor. Raylene says that when I get back on my feet I should try out for the Devil's stunt team. Says I'm a natural for the Devil's stunt team. *Besides*, she says, *they've got the best uniforms and you never have to pay for your time at the shooting range*. I'll probably have to have plastic surgery first–maybe change my finger prints, too. But I've been practicing. Practicing painting pictures of lava. Mostly red and orange, with a little black here and there. I'm pretty good, even if it's hard to get the volcanoes just right. You'd think that would be the easy part? What are volcanoes, anyway? Just exploding mountains. No big deal. But when the volcano painting isn't going too good, I like to get in the car and go for a drive. Doesn't matter where I go. Sometimes, I drive all night. Roll the windows down, listen to the wind. It sounds like nails hissing through wood. Have you ever noticed that? Maybe that's just me? I don't know. I like to drive out into the desert, way past Pahrump; watch the sun come up. Did you know there's no word for 'smile' in Latin? I read that in a book, once. Those poor Romans. At least they had swimming pools. The trouble with the desert is that it's running out of easy-to-kill prey. They say the planet is getting warmer, and it's affecting the wildlife. I love wildlife. They're not really that different from you and me. Not really. The snakes and the bugs, they just live their lives. Just do snake and bug things. They even sleep at night. Hey, I hope nothing terrible happens. That would be a shame. The snakes and the bugs. Coyotes too. All gone. They're just like us. They don't like heat. Not really. Not even in the desert. The snakes and bugs and coyotes. At least there aren't any volcanoes. Not yet. But you never know. I might drive out there one day, and there'll be nothing but lava; the wildlife all burnt-up. You never know for sure. They say everything is getting hotter. With all this damn radiation, there's no telling. But don't worry. Not about the coyotes, anyway. Coyotes are smart. They've got brains. Not like bugs and snakes. They think like us. At night, you can read their minds; you can tell what they're thinking. Sometimes even before they're thinking it. If anything happens to the coyotes, I'll let you know. Ditto, the volcanoes.

That's A Whole Other Story

In order to enjoy the fictitious sunlight, I like to get up early, right before the false dawn, in fact, before I'm able to fully remember myself, just when my arms are at their shortest. Although I may be handcuffed to this gurney, I can't help but recall my square roots, especially my father, a beat-up boxcar of a man, whose hands were the size of oil wells and whose gait was steady as a pendulum. Like most plumbers, he lived in constant fear of water. On secret occasions, he would take me aside and remind me that although I was still too young to appreciate his wisdom, every life is like a poached egg–quivering and shell-less. He relied heavily on the rules of capitalization and exhilarating brevity, which explains, I think, how he met my mother and for so many years avoided extradition. Although he was a simple man who made his living in the building trades, he had a natural, I dare say, perverse, talent for Continental philosophy. For example, he solved the infinite regress problem in cosmology by simply inquiring, *But do turtles think its humans all the way down?* His sincerity was awe-inspiring, as was his conviction that nothing mattered so much as the preservation of our homey folkways and the ever-quickening circuits of free-flowing, global capitalism. His enigmatic love for me made me feel like a concrete airplane crashed in a bonsai jungle. Once, when I realized I was receiving no tweets and was filled with a plethora of inattention due to my reckless multitasking, I resolved to live life just like my father had–as if I were a snake looking for its legs, or a fan club to which no one belongs. What better way, I thought, to glide across this mortal coil? I worked diligently to perfect a picture-perfect yell. I cultivated an undergraduate's love for high culture, including glacier museums and oppressive tribal operas. I became a master of phrenology. I even spent several weeks sublimating my higher order cognitive skills and letting my id do all the nighttime driving. And sure enough, it wasn't long before I realized that water doesn't know when it's boiling, and that around every corner there lurks an inescapable right angle. That said, some true stories are truer than others. It can't be helped. Of course, they never did find my father's bloodied body.

Friday Night Drive to Watertown

I'm wearing flammable clothing. Also wearing the inflammable clothing. You can't be too careful. Although it's not posted, I'm driving the exact speed limit. It must have snowed last night, because I just passed a house with a square snowman. Man, I tell you, those kids have real problems. I hope they get some help. Soon. You know what I always say? Don't stand on your own shoelaces. A calamity yes, but never a catastrophe. Yesterday, I bought a special, left-handed ball point pen. I thought it would help with this damned metric system. This morning, I drank some truth serum. I hate that stuff. It turns out, I have nyctophobia, but it's not covered by my insurance. Wouldn't you know it? Of course, now I want to de-activate my pet, but I have to read up on it, first. I take back everything I ever said about jellyfish. Last week, during my visit to Disney World, I threw out all my dirty laundry. Apparently, I had made other plans. I just don't understand it; my outfit looked so beautiful on the mannequin. She was wearing plaid pants and had a short husband. It kind of blew my mind. I ask you, with such a dim bulb, how was I supposed to conduct a successful interrogation? Sometimes, my mattress gets so nervous I just can't get any sleep. It's not like I planned to shoot out those car windows. Don't be alarmed. I can explain everything.

Amateur Advice

I am an expert amateur. And yet, I have nothing. There were a lot of things I could have been, but sadly, now there is no one to thank. Of course, there are always new mistakes to be made, but with little hope of compensation, it's nearly a lost art. My advice to you is to make a list of yourself and practice your sleeping skills. You must also try to dream more frequently of animals, preferably ungulates. You may wonder, *will this be on the final exam?* I can assure you my friend, it won't. Everyone already knows the answer. By the way, I hate to ruin your pitching arm, but have you noticed that wherever you go, it's not on the map? Maybe it's both a hardware AND a software problem? You know what I always say; if you don't want to see the sights, don't look out the window. Of course, every dream is momentous, no matter how large or small, even the fire ant's dream. A red apple has more genes than the human genome. Eventually, everything, flammable and inflammable, will burst into flames. I'll bet no one has ever given you the Heimlich maneuver like that before? Don't blame me. Just because I forgot to bring the cooler, doesn't mean I don't know how to have a good time. The medium is the message. But so is the xtra-large.

III.

III

Doppler Effect

Away from even the most perfect of emergencies
an ambulance can travel only so fast.
You hear the siren's swelling, red-raw wail, and wonder,
is that a still life glimpsed fleetingly,
as if from a passing train?
Of course, whatever we may say love is,
it is an echo, word-for-word,
of its dumbfounded flight.

There must be another name
for this kind of diminishing noise,
as it recedes in rapid retreat from the heart's horizon,
its distance, an emptied ocean,
its duration, foreshortened stillness.
And how, as it passes and fades,
we never think of it any longer,
all of the time.

Since Dad Left

On my street, the trees
don't know their names.

Paper boys are paper girls,
who invisibly arrive and vanish at dawn.

Our house,
the color of milk,

is surrounded by blue, shivering roses.
Its shouting windows

sealed, but un-curtained,
so the neighbors can peer

into the living room where no one lives,
as mom parades around nude, again,

to prove to the sofa and chairs from Sears
she's not dead yet, mister,

not by a goddamned long shot.

The Truth About Love

Long ago, when music was rectangular, I was voted by my senior class "most likely to survive capital punishment." Of course, there are many different kinds of love. Some are angry fun, others, a one-car funeral. Like that time we were driving across the Golden Gate Bridge and you told me that I have two different colored eyes. I realized, right then and there, we are spied upon by our own Wi-Fi. As long as I am barreling through this amnesia, I might as well mention that incident with the lesbian robots. At first, I thought it was a party trick, until you told me it was just me. How was I to know it wasn't necessary to communicate exclusively via homophones? What did you expect? I don't read music, although I do own all the Led Zeppelin Christmas albums. By the way, I don't care what color they are, Fruit Loops are all an identical flavor, and I'm willing to bet some real Hollywood money to prove it, too. Yes, I was in church when that terrible weight-lifting accident happened. The barbells were so heavy, not even Jesus could lift them. But as you know, we're always willing to forgive beauty, even if we're never prepared to forgive love. Just as time leaks from a clock, little by little, love leaks from our lives. There is nothing we can do about it. It's the just law of averages. Because everyone knows love is nothing like that.

Waiting Room View

Gray as a gull,
I am an old man now,
gruff, yearning.

Across the nearly vacant
waiting room,
one young woman,
beautifully bored,
eyes dark as Poe's raven,
peers though me.

I am a window.
There is no view.
Her gaze does not stop
at my heart.

A Bite, Not a Sting

Of course, real punishment is having to be the person you are, although frankly, it's already none of my business. As I recite this poem to your lie detector, I notice that my mouth disperses vibrant, hard-to-pin-down air, with the flavor of a multivitamin. It's like being ill and ugly cool. Whenever I'm seized by choreomania, I find it's best to confess I'm renowned for failing at next steps. Nonetheless, I tweet whatever I feel like, whenever I feel like it. You probably think that's because Elvis impersonators are a dime a dozen. But that's not true. It's like that time you told me that the mosquitoes were singing you an aria. *Believe me*, I said, while slapping myself in the face, *it's for your own good*. For better and for worse, our memories are reshaped and rewritten every time we recall an event. *Don't' be ridiculous*, you assured me, *mosquitoes don't sting*.

Your Words Are Like Heaven

Let's be honest. Language isn't everything they say it is. You may think you know what you're talking about, but you can be certain of only one thing: you'll survive only as long as you don't question whether this is a conversation you're having in your head or a disagreeable echo. Now, here's a place I know you'd love to visit, but not a place you'd want to live: *We're just down the road from Heathrow, and sometimes, as they lower their landing gear, a body falls out.* Of course, people like to find things exactly where they left them. Buckminster Fuller said, *Everybody's an astronaut*, but sadly, it's a one-way world. The sky unlocks its ghost atoms and you can't just stand there, you have to do something. Tonight, I feel like telling the truth: death is the speed limit no one can break. Nevertheless, after the funeral, I promise to call your voicemail. I've been pacing myself, although my nerves are busy as a dolphin stampede. I wonder: *what if the translator's lying to me?* Buddha exhales his slow, smoky, Mona Lisa smile, *Don't worry, my friend, there's no word for it in English.* My car swerves like a black finch, dead drunk, toward the moon's honeysuckle trough. I careen past a gang of ghosts hammering up a brand-new ghost town. They've taken out the lake of fire, then re-installed it. Ugly houses, spectacular view. Just saying.

Cyborg's Blue Quantum Love Dance

We're up all night amid the flesh puppets at the punk factory, the music's blue hammers flailing against the voltage of my impeccably simulated ulterior motives. When, above the din, you shriek *Honey, those are nearly lifelike feelings you've got there,* I yearn to whisper sweet passwords in your ear, to confess copyright- pending algorithms, to reveal my inner search terms. Then you add, *Why don't you come a little bit closer, Winston?* I'm shocked to discover you'd like to reboot me— although not here on the dance floor, of course. Although I can see you don't really want a ghost in the machine, least of all, one emitting mixed signal-to-noise while robotically moshing in the alternating current, in my heart of hearts, I'm confident there's no substitute for love's simulacrum. I hunger to set flame to the cacophonous quantum, the biochemical fabric of this mirror-ball moment, especially if you and I can reciprocally depolarize one another's neuronal bionics. You suggest that we retreat to your fervent apartment, where your collection of feral electrons and natty android equipage promises to set a tranquilizing mood for one sublime intertwining. As we leave, you warn me, *Winston, no matter how anode or cathode, human or non-, desire imitates art, and art, victorious advertising.* Undeterred, I remind you that the voltage of love's voltage runs along the truest of circuits, regardless of who's done the programming, especially in this great, unmanned land of ours. *Yes,* you reply, *thank God, operators are always standing by.*

Makes No Difference

Orange fingernails on nine of ten, one thumb missing. She's slept with two-hundred forty-one truckers, not counting her husband. When I get up enough nerve to ask her to dance, she says. *One of my legs ain't real; guess which one.* From where I stand, the rodeo-print mini-skirt can't hide anything, but I say to her, *I can't tell which is fake and which is real.* She leans in so close, I can smell the hops of the warm Budweisers, and she says to me, *When it comes to men, honey, neither can I. But like legs, it don't make no difference.*

Tattoo Lover

We squabbled,
snapping like fire crackers,
about you getting a tattoo.
A rose, a snake, a lightning bolt?
How big, how small, where should it go?

Everyone had one, even your aunt,
and then your voice dropped
to that smoky register,
as if to announce Roman ruins about to crumble:
my claim to your flesh.

Above the weather of your blood,
needles hatched meticulous blossoms,
little whorls of roses, delicate as a child's whisper,
hemming your blank nape,
pin and ink, apodictic.

A few days later, your hair gathered in my tender fist,
I stood behind you
prepared to kiss your willing wound.
The petals' sharp ink sheared my lips.
The taste of thorns, sugared sweet,
climbed my tongue's splintered stake.

A mural between us,
you revealed an art
no one can possess.

Me and Buddy at the Pink Elephant

Thursday night, me and Buddy are tossing back a few beers at the Pink Elephant, when Buddy looks up from his half-empty bottle, and with that dumbass look he gets on his face after he's been thinking about things for too long, says, "I just hate stories set in bars, don't you?"

I said, "Yeah, why do you think there's so many?"

Buddy cocks his head a little and looks at me like I've been to college or something, so I say "Maybe it's so people in the stories can get drunk."

Buddy orders me another beer, and before we know it, we're ordering each other rounds and starting to feel pretty darn good.

About midnight, three guys–they sure aren't regulars–walk in: a Rabbi, a Priest, a Pastor–which seems pretty weird, but me and Buddy don't think too much about it. We just kept to ourselves, minding our own business, and drinking more beers. Pretty soon I notice both me and Buddy are keeping our eyes peeled–secretly looking over our shoulders every once in a while, in their direction. I think we both just wanted to make sure nothing really funny happened.

Rented Tux

I wasn't sure whether I was dead or alive. Now, I know that's just black and white thinking. I may be empty for the rest of my life, or some fungible equivalent thereof, but when you've had everything taken out of you, again and again, you try to make the best of absence. Thank God, nature adores a vacuum, that I trained as a mime. Although I haven't found my voice, I sometimes hear music that isn't there. I'm taken places. The nights are clean. I sleepwalk. So what if I'm a vacant fathom? A train doesn't lay its own tracks; a book isn't written to be read by other books. There is no Roman numeral zero. When I find myself admiring perfect strangers—the way they seem so comfortable in their skins, so nonchalant—I recall that appearances can be deceiving. And the wind, the invisible wind, always arriving, always departing. Always taking itself someplace brand new.

Escape Artist

I'm a secret, like the CIA. Fortunately, a suspect is innocent until proven guilty. You've got to be honest with yourself, even if it means telling a lot of lies. You never really get used to the earthquakes. Have you noticed all the ventriloquist's dummies moving into the neighborhood? I can't explain the screams. Or the blood. Pretty soon, there will be no one on the street but cops and more cops. I guess that's the beauty of symmetry. Everything you do, you'll do once, for the last time. The bombardier's hands are the cleanest. There's something comforting about the sound of a chain saw. Don't worry. I'll be waiting for you in the parking lot.

The Traveling Salesman Problem

Like a TV shouting at an empty room,
I'm thinking loud thoughts I'm unable to name.
Molecules sort themselves into the shape of a man,
the way fallen leaves once arranged themselves
into the shape of an elm.
So many cities, so many towns,
a lifetime of suitcases, beige food.

I've ascended five thousand miles
steeped in a cappella Muzak
no eye-contact, vacant smiles.
No matter what you're selling
redemption is the shortest distance
between two points.
God ticks in every minute.
Elevator time is all there is.

This morning, when I glanced in the mirror,
it was like listening to mute crickets.
I can't help but think that self-storage is a good idea,
secure and affordable, not that many break-ins.
Can the chameleon recall its native color?

On the highway now,
vacant as a July elementary school,
I turn up the music, drive faster.
Isolated thunder storms, lonely rain,
Why does the Genie never get a wish?

True Religion

Madam X stopped laughing. At the Dirty Laundry, amid the SWAT-ness of it all, they'd run out LOL. I thought, *That's funny, it doesn't look like a Wednesday*, but my mid-life crisis had just started to gain momentum, causing me to seriously rethink my career in miniature golf. Of course, this was not my first time at the existential rodeo, but ever since the collision, I don't trust my wristwatch. Not worth a damn. The sign in the butcher shop window read BIG WIG SALE, so I collected my thoughts, and re-positioned my lei. My parents had warned me about this. *Don't swim in Mystery Lake*, they said. But what did they know? They couldn't tell whether I was lovesick or jet lagged, even on those days when I wouldn't let go of my hairless cat, Anonymous. Jesus said we have nothing to worry about, we have an after-lifetime guarantee. Who am I to disagree with God's only child? But when I joined the tiny house movement, everyone sneered, *That's so California*, as if I had bought a lavender Cadillac or chipped a piece of terrazzo from Raymond Chandler's glittering star on Hollywood Blvd. So, I told them that I rented a four-bedroom apartment at the Venus De Milo Arms. *But, Milo, what about all that swank?* they asked. I just smiled my power-hungry smile and looked lovingly in the direction of my freshly painted lawn. Like Richard Nixon, I was completely confident there was no evidence of evidence-tampering. Besides, everyone knows it all started with just one fish, one loaf.

Titanic

The indoor trees, their decorative, green-leafed gloves, reach up to the chandeliered ceiling, the way a child reaches up to her mother to say, "Please lift me up, closer to you, I want to see, I want to see the sea," and mother lifts her daughter into her arms and points to the sea, which opens toward the sky like an upturned gray umbrella, ready to catch the rain, but the mid-April day, bright as a distant, glittering shore, is rainless, and mother says, "Oh how you've grown heavy, my little one," as she lowers the child to the cabin floor and the child begins to cry, "Mother, Mother, I want to see the sea, again" and tears begin streaming down the child's white, moon-round face, like streaks of paint scumbled against an iceberg's waterline, while in the afternoon's crisp air, the trees' leaves wave at the smooth, gray sea a kind of goodbye they will, of course, never say.

Even the Trees

Why don't you go outside and get some fresh air, Randal? It's not good to stay indoors and vanish. There was no arguing with Aunt Jane. Of course, the new apparatus had arrived and was dancing, just like fun, in the living room. Each volt, an increment of folded alarm, seemed to grasp my strategic chemicals. The operating instructions however, were written in cubic cruelty. I attached the tiny bits to the grand surfaces, then activated the magnetoresistive random access memory. *There,* I thought, *at least that's taken care of.* But no sooner had I smoothed the checkered romance of its audible heroic overload, than Aunt Jane roared from the kitchen, *It's a splendid day for a hasty lifestyle emulation, don't you think, Randal?* Who in their right mind could argue with Aunt Jane? The sun was shrieking, the cat had bolted to the unwitting neighbors, and Jane had the most definitive whistle. I tell you, simply everyone looked up to her. Even the trees.

Bull-Leaping to Bach Cantata No. 54 (Stand Firm Against Sin)

I once knew a girl who sang in her sleep, hummed Bach cantatas. So pretty, the sleep-soaked notes, levitating above her pillow, her musical murmur, beckoning the night to draw closer. She was Danish, charming, traveling the Mediterranean. What did I know about music? A brash American, barely 21, flotsam in the blue latitudes where once, the minotaur lived and naked boys tumbled over the heads of bulls. In Heraklion, Bettina whispered the hot, still night to sleep, while in my tossing restlessness, all I could dream about was a rhythm section. And horns.

Mr. Wittgenstein Writes to Ms. Stein

I called you many times, but you didn't answer. This has left me no alternative, but to write you now, in order to reach you by other means. Of course, it is as difficult to say precisely what one means, as it is to mean precisely what one says. Whereof one cannot speak, thereof one must be silent. What can one say about this? What can it mean to say that one must be silent? Silence is argument carried on by other means. Silence is noiseless argument, like a city street at 2 AM, when there is much parallel parking available because there is no one there. When there is no one there—when everyone has left—there is no there, there. And there is quiet—quiet and emptiness, like a bowler hat perched on a mannequin's head. The empty streets do not speak, they only listen. If one has nothing to say, then it is imperative that one sit very still and hum, or devise something philosophical to say. My propositions are elucidatory in this way: he who understands me finally recognizes them as senseless, when he has climbed out through them, on them, over them. He must, so to speak, throw away the ladder, after he has climbed upon it. Of course, a ladder is mostly holes. Holes are mostly emptiness and silence. When all is said and done, silence is empty and holy. Silence is holiness. Holiness is empty. Unsaid, some things are better left.

Luck

That's the fastest escalator I've ever ridden. I'm not afraid of heights. As long as they're indoors. Looked through the plus-size department, but couldn't find anything I liked. There's a 7 billion dollar market in Halloween merchandise. That's what the paper said. You'd think I could find something without horizontal stripes. Took the elevator down. I only go down in elevators, never up. I told Justine my luck really isn't luck. It just looks that way. That's why I keep my money in a paper bag. Looks like an old lunch. And those killer beeps. These days, they're everywhere you go. No getting away from them. I'd wear earplugs, but I left them at church on Sunday. Pastor said we've all got a calling, but asked us to turn off our cell phones during the service. Said he didn't think the Lord needed interruptions. He smiled when he said that. I turned mine to "vibrate" in case one of my kids got into an accident. Justine–she's' the prettiest darn thing–said she felt like playing poker after church. Some days you just feel it. We went to the *Orleans* and played a few hands. The place is clean. Mostly locals go there because the atmosphere is friendly. It's low stakes. I didn't trust the dealer, though. He looked like my parole officer. I think he was wearing a wig. I hate wigs on men. Of course, you can get used to almost anything, if you concentrate. Like those ventriloquists. They're great concentrators. Hardly move their lips. And those dummies; it's not easy with someone else's words coming out of your mouth. Like that time in court. Sure, I knew I was an accomplice, but I didn't plan the thing. I was just the driver. Didn't even use a stolen car. Probably should have. Jack was the one that said there was a lot of money in there. Jack's so smart. At least he thinks so. But what good did it do him? Got an even 20 for arson of an occupied structure. Thank goodness everybody got out. The place burned down in about a minute. Everybody got out. Everybody, but one. That's what I call real luck.

A Girl like You

Tonight, I'm waiting for the world to come to me. In the meantime, I hear the drums of car doors slamming, airtight thuds. They're not just noises, but symbols, a fact that tells me the time we spend in the dark is a Muzak-filled waiting room. Yes, I know, it's an improbable theory, but what if it's true, like viruses before their discovery? Just because something isn't real, doesn't' mean it isn't true. Take, for example, anesthesia. The unconscious mind was discovered to be in many cases a lot healthier than the conscious mind; wild, unruly, primitive and savage, yet performing remarkable athletic feats, which can neither be denied nor confirmed. For example, when I show up at the company party with my trophy-breasted wife, the room fills with spectacular whispering, *Is she with a boy or a life-sized midget?* Then, like a force occupying a defeated nation, I realize I must become the lies I tell. What are the chances? People like to find things exactly where they (last) left them. I suppose this is human nature, like a bustling jungle filled with paranoid chimps. Although it may be difficult to picture this, try to imagine an unforgivable surprise designed by committee. Of course, Paris is a great place to change planes as you're on the way to somewhere where it really counts. It's simply magical: extinct buildings; copyrighted earthquakes; potholes designed by Louis XIV; and from the top of the Eiffel Tower, a world-renowned view of *tromp l'oeil*, where you simply must put 2 and 2 together. Well, I don't mean "you" exactly, I mean "one". "One" must put 2 and 2 together, even if your watch may be a little slow. If there is one thing that physics has taught us, it's that the Big Bang is not a double entendre. It's not like I haven't' warned you about this, before. Later, you won't be able to remember if we even exchanged a kiss—a real kiss. Consequently, for my next trick, I will need a volunteer. A girl like you. Just like you. But not you.

ABOUT THE AUTHOR

Brad Rose was born and raised in southern California, and lives in Boston. He is a Pushcart Prize nominee in fiction, a 2013 recipient of Camroc Press Review's, Editor's Favorite Poetry Award, and the 2014 winner of *unFold Magazine's* "FIVE (5) Contest" for his found poem "Signs of Reincarnation at Le Parker Meridian Hotel, NY, NY." His poetry and fiction have appeared in *The Los Angeles Times, Boston Literary Magazine, The Baltimore Review, San Pedro River Review, Off the Coast, Third Wednesday, Right Hand Pointing, Midwest Quarterly, The Potomac, Santa Fe Literary Review, The Common Line Journal, The Molotov Cocktail, Sleetmagazine, Monkeybicycle, Camroc Press Review, MadHat Lit, Burning Word,* and other publications. Links to his poetry and fiction can be found at: http://bradrosepoetry.blogspot.com/

www.ingramcontent.com/pod-product-compliance
Lightning Source LLC
Chambersburg PA
CBHW072018170626
46813CB00005B/2182